Also by June Hampson

Trust Nobody
Broken Bodies
Damaged Goods
Fatal Cut
Jail Bait
Fighting Dirty

A Mother's Journey

A Mother's Journey

JUNE HAMPSON

First published in Great Britain in 2012 by Orion Books,
an imprint of The Orion Publishing Group Ltd
Orion House, 5 Upper Saint Martin's Lane
London WC2H 9EA

An Hachette UK Company

1 3 5 7 9 10 8 6 4 2

A CIP catalogue record for this book
is available from the British Library.

ISBN (Hardback) 978 1 4091 3369 8
ISBN (Trade Paperback) 978 1 4091 3370 4

Typeset by Deltatype Ltd, Birkenhead, Merseyside

Printed in Great Britain by Clays Ltd, St Ives plc

The Orion Publishing Group's policy is to use papers
that are natural, renewable and recyclable products and
made from wood grown in sustainable forests. The logging
and manufacturing processes are expected to conform to
the environmental regulations of the country of origin.

www.orionbooks.co.uk

I have trod the upward and the downward slope;
I have endured and done in the days before;
I have longed for all, and bid farewell to hope;
And I have lived and loved, and closed the door.

Robert Louis Stevenson

Acknowledgements

I am indebted to Natalie Braine and that grand team at Orion. Also to Geoffrey Boxall who came up with the idea.

Prologue

1962

'There's a bloke gonna come in any minute an' I ain't in Gosport an' you don't know me, Bert, got it?'

'You, the top prossie in Gosport, don't want to see a bloke?'

Bert was frying bacon at the gas stove, forking it over so it cooked evenly. He stopped smiling when Vera desperately cut in with, '*Please, Bert. I'm not here!*'

Vera didn't dare stay any longer in the near-deserted caff. She flew back up the wooden stairs to her room at the top of the lodging house adjoining the caff and peeked out of the window.

She shivered violently as the man's broad-shouldered body strode purposefully along the brightly lit pavement towards the caff.

It was obvious he'd come from the ferry. Suppose she'd been on her regular pitch there near the taxi rank? Suppose he'd seen her?

She dropped the net curtain back in place and looked down at the floor.

Her mackerel-coloured cat wound himself in a figure of eight around her feet encased in high-heeled mules. His fur was softer than the slippers' marabou trim.

I

'If I 'adn't let you in, Kibbles, an' looked out the window, I'd never 'ave spotted 'im.' Despite her soft words her heart was hammering. She tried to put the man out of her mind and concentrate on the cat she loved fiercely.

She bent down and picked up the weighty feline, who immediately began filling the room with his throaty purr.

'That man ruined my life. And I hoped I'd never see 'im again,' she whispered.

Yet her first thought had been to go down and give him a mouthful, scratch his eyes out maybe. She was after all a Gosport girl and Gosport girls don't take wrongs lightly. But Bert wouldn't thank her for causing a ruckus in his caff and she wasn't going to brawl in the street like some common tart.

Her heart still hadn't stopped its fluttering and she realised she was too upset to behave rationally. She needed time to think.

Still carrying the cat she walked to the wooden draining board and set Kibbles down in front of a saucer filled to the brim with sardines. Another saucer held his milk. He began to eat as she watched him.

This room was her refuge.

At the top of the building, it looked down to North Street and along North Cross Street and over Murphy's hardware shop where you could buy anything from a nail to a rose bush. Then the view swept across to the ferry pontoon where squat boats transferred passengers across the strip of murky, smelly Solent water to Portsmouth.

Vera took a deep breath in an attempt to calm her nerves.

She was trying hard not to think of Alfred below in the caff quite possibly interrogating Bert. She didn't want to think about what had happened that fateful day of the party but it all came back to her as vividly as if it was happening now.

Vera's skirt was pushed up. She couldn't move. His bulk had her pinned to the scullery floor and she could feel the strange slippery heat of him. Grunting sounds came from him as he fumbled and tore one handed at her clothes. She was on the floor inches away from the grease-stained gas oven, its smell of years of burned fat sickening her. She wanted to scream but his other hand now completely covered her mouth. And then he pushed into her and was moving inside her and it hurt.

She had been only fourteen.

Now she was thirty-five and Alfred Lovell, the man who'd caused so much pain in her life and who she'd never thought she'd see again, was downstairs.

What had brought him back to Gosport?

The only way to find out was to go down and listen.

She kicked off her hard-soled mules and opened her door. She stepped out and began creeping past the other rented rooms and back down the stairs.

Crouching on a step where she was sure she couldn't be seen, Vera hugged her nylon-clad knees close to her body. She prayed no one would need to use the lavatory and chance upon her sitting there and call out to her by name.

Even from the stairway she was aware of his almost forgotten spicy aftershave wafting up towards her.

Her body clenched as she heard his voice.

'I need to talk to Vera.'

Vera leaned forward and could just make out those broad shoulders, the strong neck and the glossy dark moustache, now threaded with grey, above full lips. His suntan only added to his good looks.

His piercing blue eyes were searching Bert's face for answers. Bert was wiping plates, making each dish glitter with cleanliness.

Silently she willed Bert to tell Alfred nothing.

'She's not 'ere tonight.' *Bless you, Bert*, she thought.

'Later on? Will she return later?'

Bert moved an overflowing glass ashtray to the other side of the Formica table. It was a studied movement, like he was thinking hard.

Vera counted just three customers. It was well past twelve and, even though the summer evening had been warm, Gosport had closed down for the night.

'Dunno.' Bert now began the laborious business of rolling up his shirt sleeves. 'What d'you want to know for? An' what's your name?'

'Alfred Lovell.' The man shifted his bulk from one foot to the other. Vera could sense his impatience. She remembered he had always been like that, irritated when things didn't go his way.

'Does she live here?' He tapped one foot on the wooden floor. 'If not, give me her address. I've heard you and she are pals.'

'Do I look like I come up the Solent in a bucket? If I am her pal I can't just give out her details, can I? That's supposing I knows 'em.' Bert hooked his thumbs into his braces and met Alfred's glare unblinkingly.

'I've come halfway around the world to see Vera, from Australia, to be exact. Not seen her for years, see? Though that's between me and her and has nothing to do with you.'

'That's as may be. Or you might just be stringing me a line, an' I *do* like to look out for our Vera. Very well thought of is our Vera. I'd be a mug to take you at your word, wouldn't I? Anyway, she's not 'ere.'

Vera held her breath as Alfred leaned closer to Bert. What if Alfred turned nasty? After all, he'd hurt her, hadn't he?

4

But he pulled back and Vera breathed a silent sigh of relief.

It wasn't that Bert couldn't take care of himself. He'd been a bit of a gangster in his former days so was well used to dealing with slippery customers. But the younger man had the advantage of physical fitness.

'Tell you what, mate. Why don't you jot your address down 'ere?' Bert fished in his greasy white apron pocket and pulled out a small stained notebook. He slid it along the table. Attached to the spiral binder by a piece of grubby string was a stub of pencil.

Alfred Lovell wrote on the pad and passed it back to Bert. Vera could still feel the tension in the air.

'If I don't hear from her in a week, I'll be back.'

And then his voice went quiet so Vera had to strain her ears to listen. 'When you see her, tell her Jen's dead.'

Vera heard the main door's bell chime its tinny sound as he made his way out.

Still Vera crouched there. So his wife, Jennifer, was dead was she? Alfred Lovell had lost his meal ticket. Vera, frightened the man might return, was too scared to move.

But he'd gone. The man who was constantly in her dreams and caused her to wake up crying and sweating had left.

Vera measured every man by Alfred Lovell and once more he was back in her life.

She held on to the banister and shakily pulled herself into an upright position. A cloud of her favourite perfume, Californian Poppy, rose with her and she breathed it deeply as though its scent could comfort her.

When she reached the bottom stair she fluffed up the ruffles on her red silk blouse and ran her fingers around the wide black plastic belt at the waist of her tight black skirt.

'He's left then?'

Bert was sitting at the table. He looked up at her voice. He'd lit a Woodbine and was scrutinising the address on the piece of paper. A fug of cigarette smoke hung around him.

'You're shivering,' he said. 'You ain't in command of yourself, are you?' Vera shook her head. Bert had done his best always to look out for her. He was a true friend in every way. Sometimes he knew her better than she knew herself.

'He's gone out the door but not out of your life.' Bert held out the paper with the address and Vera took it from him as though it was contaminated.

'Thank you for lying for me,' she said quietly.

'I didn't so much lie as bend the truth. I could tell by the cut of his clothes and his suntan that he wasn't a john. Anyway, you ain't never brought a john back to the caff in all the time you've lived here. Couldn't for the life of me see you starting now.' He took a deep pull on his cigarette then stubbed it out in the ashtray. 'Gosport's favourite prostitute you might be but when I sensed you hiding at the top of the stairs …'

'Do you think he knew I was there?' Vera asked worriedly.

'No.'

She sat down at the table. The caff was empty now. Bert got up and went over to the main door and slid the bolt along and turned the sign to closed.

'I'll clear up in the mornin'.' He walked to the now silent jukebox and pulled out its electric plug. 'Let's get out of this goldfish bowl,' Bert said with a wave towards the glass windows. 'Never know who's outside looking in.'

He turned off the lights so there was only the thin gleam from the streetlamp illuminating the stairs.

He held open the door from the caff that led into the hallway.